Very Lulu

The (Mostly) True Story of a Training School Dropout

words by
Stephanie Campisi

pictures by
Jessica Gibson

sourcebooks jabberwocky

Sniff
Sniff

To Mum and Juzzie, who gave me a childhood full of love (and dogs).
—SC

To my mom, who has always been supportive throughout my personal art journey.
—JG

Text © 2019 by Stephanie Campisi
Illustrations © 2019 by Jessica Gibson
Cover and internal design © 2019 by Sourcebooks

Sourcebooks and the colophon are registered trademarks of Sourcebooks, Inc.

All rights reserved.

The artwork was rendered in Photoshop and with a Wacom Cintiq tablet.

Published by Sourcebooks Jabberwocky, an imprint of Sourcebooks Kids
P.O. Box 4410, Naperville, Illinois 60567-4410
(630) 961-3900
sourcebookskids.com

Library of Congress Cataloging-in-Publication Data is on file with the publisher.

Source of Production: 1010 Printing Asia Limited, North Point, Hong Kong, China
Date of Production: May 2019
Run Number: 5014956

Printed and bound in China.
OGP 10 9 8 7 6 5 4 3 2 1

Lulu was a free spirit.

She loved
to spin,

and roll,

and lean out the
car window.

Everywhere that Lulu went
she sniffed out fun.

Sniff
Sniff

She had a
nose for it.

Actually, she had a nose for everything.

And that was how she ended up here.

"Well!" said the officer. "She's very…"
"She's very Lulu," said Lulu's handler.

The other dogs were not very Lulu at all.

They could count,

and speak on command,

and tell left from right.

And they only sniffed
what they were told to sniff.

OFFICE

Lulu sniffed anything
she wanted.

Like doughnuts, potted plants, and socks.

The officer took Lulu's handler aside.
"Do you really think Lulu has what
it takes? She's very…"

"She's very Lulu,"
said Lulu's handler.

After lunch, the officer decided to have a talk with Lulu. "Lulu, can you be more like the other dogs? You don't want to fail, do you?"

Lulu had not known a dog could fail anything.

So she tried.

She really did.

The other dogs ran obstacle courses.

But Lulu *was* an obstacle.

"Lulu!"

The other dogs fetched evidence.

Lulu had to *be* fetched.

"Lulu!"

The other dogs tracked scents.

The officer took Lulu's handler aside.
"Maybe we should get some help with Lulu. She's very…"

"She's very Lulu,"
said Lulu's handler.

Still, they tried.
They really did.

They brought Lulu treats.

They brought Lulu toys.

They even brought Lulu someone to talk to.

But Lulu was still very Lulu.

Mostly.
Lulu was beginning to miss her old life.

She missed being able to
slide and scramble and tug
on ropes.

She missed
sniffing out
fun.

The officer took Lulu's handler aside.
"Do you really think this is the job
for Lulu? She's very..."

"Unhappy," agreed Lulu's handler.

"But I know a job she's perfect for..."

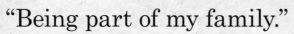

"Being part of my family."

And that was how she ended up here.

The Real Lulu!

Very Lulu is based on the real-life story of Lulu, a black Labrador who was recruited into a CIA training program. A few weeks into training, Lulu stopped showing interest in her work. It became clear that Lulu wasn't enjoying herself, and her trainers agreed that perhaps this wasn't the job for her.

When dogs leave the CIA's training programs, their handlers get the chance to adopt them. Just like the Lulu in this book, the real-life Lulu was adopted by her handler and now spends her days as a beloved family pet.

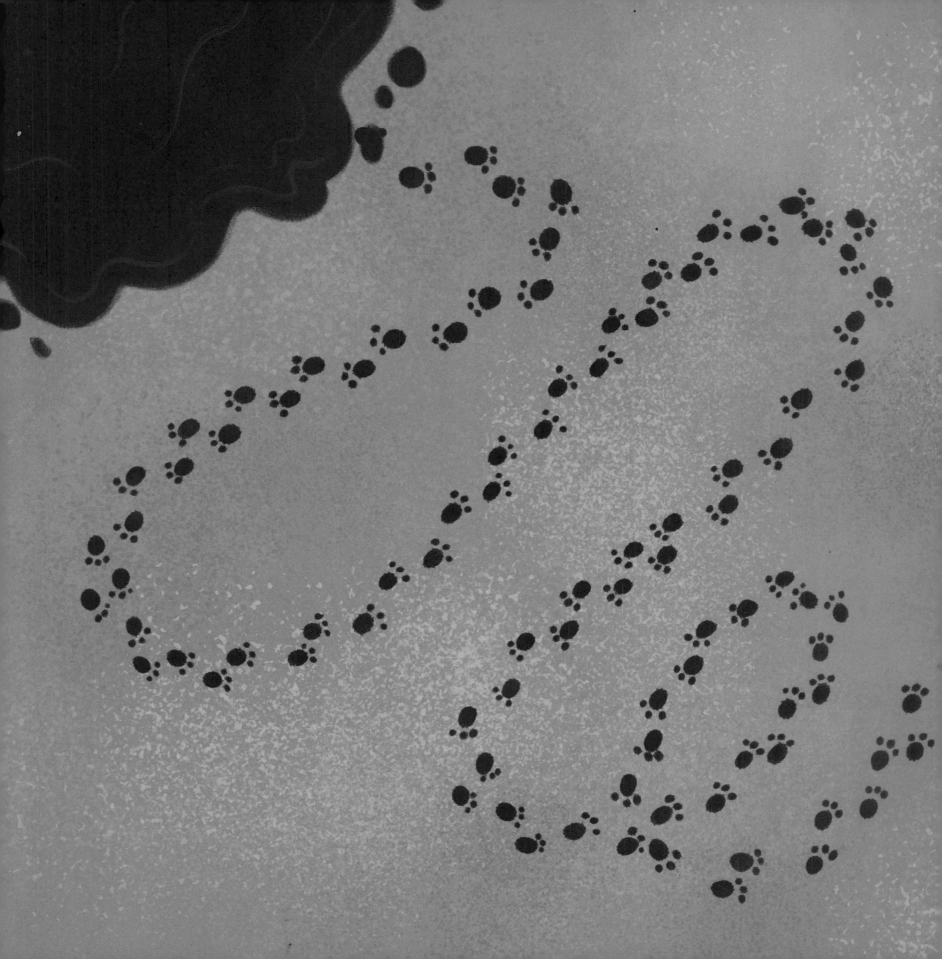